Usborne Farmyard Tales
Sticker Stories

The
Grumpy Goat

Heather Amery

Illustrated by Stephen Cartwright

Language consultant: Betty Root
Series editor: Jenny Tyler

How to use this book

This book tells a story about the Boot family. They live on Apple Tree Farm.
Some words in the story have been replaced by pictures.
Find the stickers that match these pictures and stick them over the top.
Each sticker has the word with it to help you read the story.

Some of the big pictures have pieces missing.
Find the stickers with the missing pieces to finish the pictures.

A yellow duck is hidden in every picture. When you have found
the duck you can put a  sticker on the page.

This is Apple Tree Farm.

Mrs. Boot, the farmer, lives on Apple Tree Farm.

She has two
children
called Poppy and Sam.

She also has a
dog
called Rusty.

2

Ted works on the farm.

He tells  and Sam to clean the goat's

Poppy

shed. "Will she let us?" asks Sam. "She's such a

grumpy ."

goat

3

The goat's name is Gertie.

The children go into her pen. She butts Sam and he

drops his  broom . Sam, Poppy and Rusty

run out through the 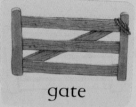 gate .

4

Poppy shuts the gate.

The  broom is still in the pen. They

must get Gertie out of her pen so they can get to

her ![shed]. "I have an idea," says Sam.

Sam gets a bag of bread.

"Come on Gertie. Nice ,"

he says. Gertie eats the bread. She eats the

as well. But she stays in her pen.

6

"Let's try some fresh grass," says Poppy.

She pulls up some  and drops

it by the 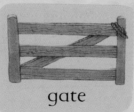. Gertie eats it but

trots back into her pen.

7

"I have another idea," says Sam.

"Gertie doesn't butt Ted. She wouldn't butt me

if I looked like ." He runs off again.

Ted

"Where are you going?" asks .

8

Poppy

Sam comes back.

I found the duck!

He's wearing Ted's old  and

coat

 . Sam goes into the pen but

hat

Gertie still butts him. Poppy laughs.

9

Poppy gets a long rope.

They go into the pen.   tries to throw

Poppy

the   **rope**   over Gertie's head. She misses

Gertie but nearly catches Sam.

Gertie is very angry.

She chases them all.  Rusty

runs out of the pen and Gertie follows him.

"She's out! Quick, shut the gate," shouts   Sam.

Sam and Poppy clean out Gertie's pen.

They sweep up the old straw and put it in the

wheelbarrow . Then they spread out fresh

straw.

Rusty watches them work.

12

"Come on, Gertie," says Sam.

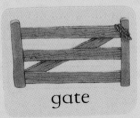
I found the duck!

"You can go back now." Poppy opens the

gate. Gertie trots back into her pen.

"Hooray," shouts Sam.

"You are a grumpy old goat," says Poppy.

I found the

"We've cleaned out your  shed and

you're still grumpy," says Sam.

Gertie

just looks at them.

14

The next morning, Poppy and Sam meet Ted.

"Come and look at Gertie now," says  .

Ted

They all go to the goat pen.

Rusty

goes with them.

I found the duck!

Gertie has a little kid.

"Oh, isn't it sweet," says Poppy. "Gertie doesn't

look grumpy now," says  Sam .

Cover design and digital manipulation by Nelupa Hussain

This edition first published in 2005 by Usborne Publishing Ltd, Usborne House, 83-85 Saffron Hill, London EC1N 8RT, England. www.usborne.com
Copyright © 2005 Usborne Publishing Ltd. The name Usborne and the devices ⬙ ⬙ are Trade Marks of Usborne Publishing Ltd. All rights reserved.
No part of this publication may be reproduced, stored in a retrieval system, or transmitted in any form or by any means, electronic, mechanical,
photocopying, recording or otherwise without the prior permission of the publisher. First published in America 2005. U.E. Printed in Malaysia.